First published 1986 by
Walker Books Ltd
87 Vauxhall Walk
London SE11 5HJ

This edition published 2001

2 4 6 8 10 9 7 5 3

© 1986 Colin West

This book has been typeset in Optima

Printed in Hong Kong

British Library Cataloguing in Publication Data:
a catalogue record for this book
is available from the British Library

ISBN 0-7445-8257-1

"Pardon?" said the giraffe

Colin West

WALKER BOOKS

AND SUBSIDIARIES

LONDON • BOSTON • SYDNEY

"What's it like up there?"
asked the frog
as he hopped on the ground.

"Pardon?"
said the
giraffe.

"What's it like up there?"
asked the frog
as he hopped on the lion.

"Pardon?"
said the
giraffe.

"What's it like up there?"
   asked the frog
   as he hopped on the hippo.

"Pardon?" said the giraffe.

"What's it like up there?"
  asked the frog
   as he hopped on the elephant.

"Pardon?" said the giraffe.

"What's it like up there?"
asked the frog
as he hopped on the giraffe.

"It's nice up here, thank you,"
  said the giraffe,
"but you're tickling my nose
  and I think I'm going to..."

A-A-A-TISHOOOOO

"What's it like down there?" asked the giraffe.

"Pardon?" said the frog.

COLIN WEST says that the idea for **_"Pardon?" said the giraffe_** came to him because he wanted to write a story about animals of different heights. He says, "A giraffe is the natural choice for a tall animal, while a frog provided me with a good, cheeky, small character. 'What's it like up there?' is a phrase rather tall people often have to put up with. In my story I think the giraffe can hear the question perfectly well, but she is determined to wear out the rude frog as he hops higher and higher."

Colin West enjoys working on all types of book, including poetry and story books. He is the author/illustrator of many books, including the Giggle Club titles _Buzz, Buzz, Buzz, Went Bumble-bee_; _"I Don't Care!" Said the Bear_; _One Day in the Jungle_ and _"Only Joking!" Laughed the Lobster_ as well as the jungle tales _"Go tell it to the toucan!"_; _"Have you seen the crocodile?"_; _"Not me," said the monkey_ and _"Hello, great big bullfrog!"_ Colin lives in Epping, Essex.

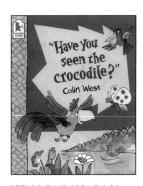
ISBN 0-7445-8254-7 (pb)

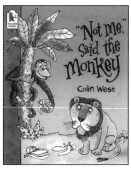
ISBN 0-7445-8256-3 (pb)

ISBN 0-7445-8255-5 (pb)

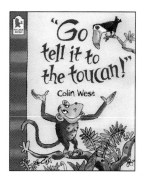
ISBN 0-7445-8253-9 (pb)